ROXIE MUNRO

HATCH!

Marshall Cavendish Children

To the birder in my family, Suzanne Munro Gubbings

Many thanks to Caleb E. Gordon, Ph.D.,
Senior Avian Ecologist at Pandion Systems Inc. in Gainesville, Florida,
for his expert review of this manuscript.

Did You Know?

Answers:

Birds much taller than any human being: Ostriches
Birds that can fit on a child's palm: Bee hummingbirds
Birds with nests that weigh as much as a car: Bald eagles
Birds with nests that are smaller than a walnut: Some hummingbirds
Birds that can't fly: Penguins, ostriches, some cormorants, kiwis, and others
Birds that can't walk: Frigate birds and most hummingbirds
Birds that can stay underwater for more than fifteen minutes: Emperor penguins
Birds that sleep while flying: Albatrosses, some swifts, and others
Birds that can fly one hundred miles per hour: Peregrine falcons, some swifts, red-breasted mergansers
Birds with twelve-foot wingspans: Wandering albatrosses
Birds that can fly as high as a jet plane (eight miles up): Bar-headed geese
Birds that migrate twenty-five thousand miles in a year: Arctic terns

Text and illustrations copyright © 2011 by Roxie Munro

Marshall Cavendish Corporation, 99 White Plains Road, Tarrytown, NY 10591
www.marshallcavendish.us/kids

Library of Congress Cataloging-in-Publication Data
Munro, Roxie.
Hatch! / by Roxie Munro.—1st ed.
p. cm.
ISBN 978-0-7614-5882-1
1. Birds—Eggs—Juvenile literature. 2. Birds—Behavior—Juvenile literature. I. Title.
QL675.M86 2011
598—dc22
2010021297

The illustrations are rendered in India ink and colored ink.
Book design by Anahid Hamparian
Editor: Marilyn Brigham

Printed in China (E)
First edition
10 9 8 7 6 5 4 3 2 1

 Marshall Cavendish
Children

Birds are some of the most fascinating creatures on Earth.

They live all over the world—from the frozen polar regions to sizzling hot deserts. Bird pirates steal food from other animals, and scavenger birds eat animals that are already dead. Birds make all sorts of sounds—from singing to honking to hooting and whistling. Birds have been around for a long time, too. Fossils with feathers have been found that date back to one hundred and fifty million years ago. Over nine thousand species of birds currently live on Earth.

All birds lay eggs, and most build nests. Many eggs are white or light-colored, but others are dark or have squiggles, dots, and other markings. Some eggs hatch in under an hour, while others can take up to two days. You'll see lots of eggs in *Hatch!* Try to guess what kind of bird these eggs come from. When you turn the page, you'll find out the answer and see the bird and its nest in its habitat.

Did You Know?

There are birds much taller than any human being; there are birds that can fit on a child's palm. Birds can make nests that weigh as much as a car or are smaller than a walnut. Some birds can't fly, others can't walk, and some can stay underwater for more than fifteen minutes. There are birds that sleep while flying and others that can fly one hundred miles per hour. There are birds with twelve-foot wingspans, birds that can fly as high as a jet plane (eight miles up), and birds that migrate twenty-five thousand miles in a year—the circumference of the Earth. (See facing page to find out which birds these are.)

Can you guess whose eggs these are?

They belong to a songbird whose name was inspired by the male's bright colors, which resemble the coat of arms of a seventeenth-century Maryland governor. A Major League Baseball team adopted its name and colors from this bird. The female weaves a complicated three-layered basketlike hanging nest made of fiber, hair, yarn, and fine grasses, and usually lays three or four eggs. The nest is attached to forked tree branches, generally far out from the trunk, making it hard for climbing predators to reach.

BALTIMORE ORIOLES eat fruit, insects, nectar, and are among the few birds that like to eat hairy caterpillars. They sometimes spread their wings and tails and sit on top of an anthill. This is a behavior called "anting" and is practiced by over two hundred bird species worldwide. Both parents feed the little ones, which have been called the "crybabies of the world" because of their constant cries for food. Baltimore orioles are found in North America, east of the Rockies, and often migrate to Central and South America in the winter, flying mainly at night.

Also in this woodland habitat: coyote, red-tailed hawk, porcupine, turtle

Can you guess whose eggs these are?

The bird that lays these eggs is found on every continent except Antarctica. The babies that hatch are cared for by both parents. The eggs, usually two in a clutch, are white, so they can be seen in the dark. These birds are nocturnal, which means they hunt at night. They are raptors, birds of prey. Their soft, velvety feathers cover even their legs and feet, which helps muffle sound. The birds fly in almost complete silence through the dark, pouncing on victims. To learn hunting skills, the young stay with their parents for months.

GREAT HORNED OWLS are big—almost two feet tall—
and have powerful talons that can crush prey in an instant.
Because of their fierce nature and willingness to pursue animals
even larger than themselves, these owls are sometimes called the
"tigers in the sky." Their eyes point directly forward but, unlike
human eyes, they don't rotate. A very flexible neck compensates
for this—a quick two-hundred-seventy-degree swirl, and the
owl can see what's going on behind its back. With their call,
Whooo-whooo-whoooooo-who-who, they're often
referred to as "hoot owls."

Also in this forest habitat: bats, rabbit, deer, raccoon

Can you guess whose egg this is?

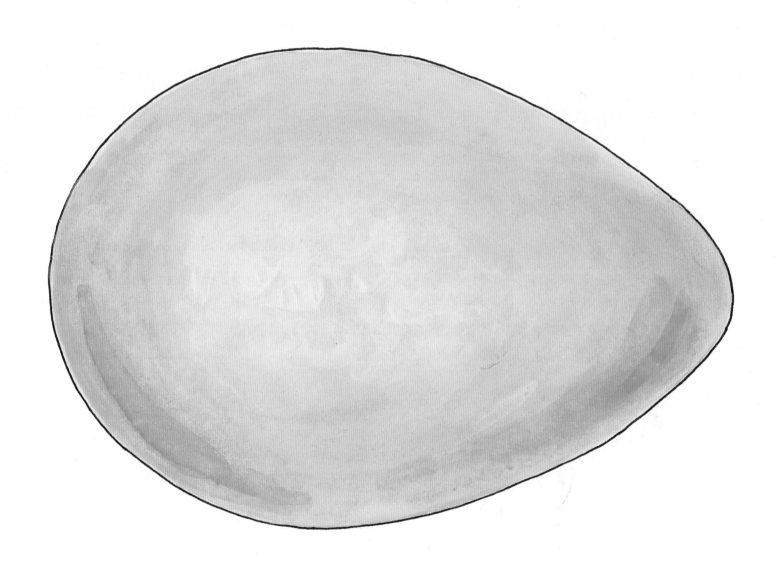

This egg belongs to a bird that can't fly but is an excellent swimmer. It can stay underwater for up to eighteen minutes and dive to depths of more than seven hundred feet. It doesn't leave the ocean except to molt or breed in huge colonies of thousands of birds. The mother travels to the sea to feed, and the father incubates one single egg. The male can't eat while taking care of the egg and may lose up to a third of his body weight. Only after the mom returns can he go back to sea— sometimes sixty miles away—to feed.

EMPEROR PENGUINS have dense, oily feathers and thick layers of fat to keep them warm in the coldest climate on Earth. They have webbed feet and wings like flippers. Almost four feet tall, emperor penguins are the largest of all seventeen penguin species. They're clumsy walkers. To move across the snow, they'll sometimes slide on their stomachs like a toboggan. Male emperor penguins incubate a single egg for nine weeks, keeping it balanced on their feet, pressing it against their tummies. An emperor's greatest fear is running into a leopard seal, a predator that lurks near the edges of the ice, ready for the kill.

Also in this polar habitat: leopard seal, snow petrels, south polar skua, Weddell seals

Can you guess whose eggs these are?

These eggs belong to a bird mom who lays one egg a
day for twelve days (or until the clutch, or brood, is complete).
And every hour during incubation, she turns the eggs to keep them
at an even temperature. This is the only species that can sleep on the
water with one eye open. These birds sleep close together in groups,
called "rafts." The male's green head, yellow bill, and black rump is
a familiar sight for many people living in North America,
where there are almost ten million of these birds.

MALLARD ducklings can swim as soon as they hatch. Their webbed feet work like paddles in the water and are good for walking on soft, marshy ground. Their wide, flat bill sifts food from the water. Mallards are "dabblers" rather than "diver" ducks because they feed on the surface of the water and don't dive. Mallards can spring straight up from the water, while diving ducks need to gain momentum for takeoff—running across the water a short distance before flying. There are one hundred and fifty species of ducks, and mallards are the most abundant duck species on Earth.

Also in this wetland habitat: great blue heron, alligator, osprey, frog

Can you guess whose eggs these are?

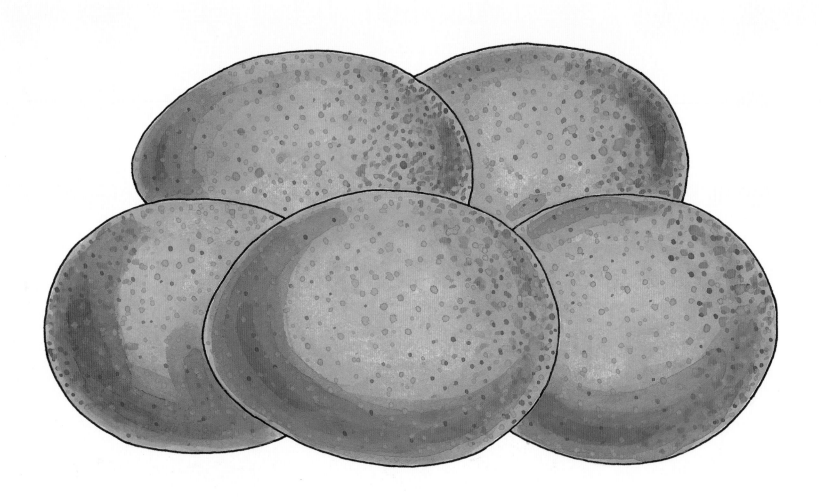

These eggs belong to the state bird of Arizona. The nest is built in a large cactus or thick shrub or tree; the size and shape of a football, it is made with grass and straw and lined with feathers. The female incubates the eggs, usually four or five, while the male builds several more nests nearby. These nests are "dummies," or "decoys," and are made to confuse predators. After about two weeks, the eggs hatch and both parents feed the hatchlings.

A CACTUS WREN never drinks. A true bird of the desert, it gets almost all of its water from food (insects, such as ants, beetles, grasshoppers, wasps; seeds; and sometimes tree frogs or lizards). Cactus wrens lay two or three clutches a season. They first set up a nest with a tunnel-like entrance that faces away from the cold winds of early spring. During the hot summer, the nest is placed to expose the opening to cooling breezes. Sometimes, a baby from a first clutch will babysit a brother or sister from a later brood.

Also in this desert habitat: turkey vultures, rattlesnake, tarantula, horned lizard, coyote

Can you guess whose eggs these are?

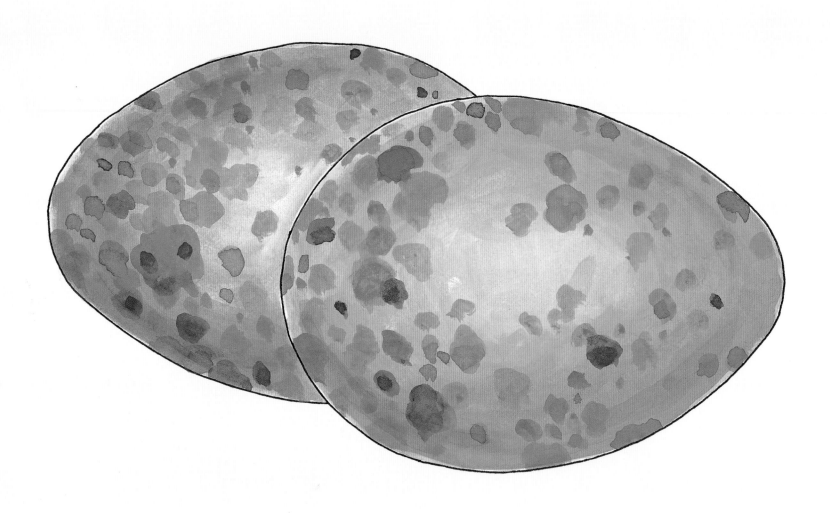

They belong to a bird that spends most of its life at
sea, far from shore. This bird drinks salt water, sleeps while
drifting on the waves, and comes ashore only for the nesting
period. The eggs, one to three in a clutch, have a lot of variety—
different colors and patterns—so parents can tell them
apart from the hundreds, sometimes thousands, of other
eggs in the same nesting colony. Both parents help
build the nest, incubate the eggs, and feed
the babies.

BLACK-LEGGED KITTIWAKES are the only gulls
that dive and swim underwater. They nest with many
other birds on narrow cliff ledges—sometimes so narrow that the
birds face the cliff front with their feet on solid ground and their tails
sticking out over the edge. The hind toe on the foot of this bird is just a
tiny bump, giving the bird its scientific name, *Rissa tridactyla*—the
second word means "three-toed." (Most birds have four toes on
each foot.) But the bird's common name comes from its
call, a shrill *Kittee-wa-aaake, kitte-wa-aaake.*

Also in this coastal habitat: whale, peregrine falcon, seals, arctic fox

Can you guess whose egg this is?

This giant egg, the world's largest, is up to
seven inches long and weighs approximately
two and a half pounds. That's the size of more than
twenty hen's eggs. The adult bird is the world's tallest
at up to nine feet, and the heaviest, weighing about three
hundred and fifty pounds. Its wings help the bird to keep
its balance when running, but their main use is for
display and courtship. When a male wants to impress a
female, he'll hold his wings out while stomping his
feet. This bird has long, powerful legs and is the
fastest-running two-legged animal on Earth.
But it can't fly.

The OSTRICH, found in the wilds of Africa, is a terrific sprinter that clocks in at sixty miles per hour—faster than a racehorse—and is able to keep running for thirty minutes without stopping. The male scrapes out a shallow pit, and several females lay clutches of about ten eggs apiece in a communal nest. But only one dominant mom incubates them, rejecting some of the others' eggs. After the babies are hatched, the mom, who is sand-colored, takes care of them during the day. Dads care for them at night—their darker coloration helps camouflage the nests from predators, such as hyenas, jackals, and vultures.

Also in this grassland habitat: jackal, zebras, giraffes, hippos

Can you guess whose eggs these are?

About the size of a pea, these are the smallest of all bird eggs. The bird that lays them is only three and a half inches long and weighs just an eighth of an ounce (about as much as two pennies). But it can beat its wings fifty-two times a second and has a heartbeat of twelve hundred times a minute! And this bird is fast, averaging twenty-five miles per hour. To maintain its body weight, it has to eat up to fifteen times an hour. The name of this species comes from the buzzing sound created as it flies.

The female RUBY-THROATED HUMMINGBIRD weaves a tiny nest. Only two inches across and one inch deep, the nest is held together with spider-web silk and, on the outside, decorated with lichen. The hummingbird has very short legs and can barely walk, but when it flies it's a dazzling performer. It can hover, fly upside down, and even fly backward, thanks to a shoulder swivel joint. In the fall, these brilliant, jewel-colored birds migrate to Central America, sometimes crossing the Gulf of Mexico in a single flight.

Also in this backyard habitat: robin, gray squirrel, red-headed woodpecker, monarch butterfly

Can you guess whose eggs these are?

These eggs, a clutch of one to three, belong to a bird that lives only in North America. This bird can fly to an altitude of ten thousand feet, higher than many mountains. Its wings are long and broad, good for soaring—flying or gliding with little effort. Carrying branches or sticks in their beaks or with their feet, both parents build an enormous nest in a tree or on a cliff ledge, renewing and adding to it each year. The largest nest ever measured was twenty feet deep, ten feet wide, and weighed two tons—more than a car.

BALD EAGLES are birds of prey (raptors). They have strong talons (claws), powerful beaks to rip food into bite-sized chunks, and wingspans of up to seven feet. Bald eagles are not bald; they have white feathers on their heads. The "bald" part of their name comes from an old English word meaning "white." These birds will chase other birds and steal their food, sometimes catching a fish in midair after a frightened bird dropped it. There are sixty-three species of eagles. Since 1783, the bald eagle has been the national symbol of the United States of America. Until 1995, the bald eagle was listed as an "Endangered" species in many states. In 1995 the status of the bird was changed to "Threatened." But it is still vulnerable.

Also in this lake habitat: brown bear, geese, pileated woodpecker, red fox

Find Out More about Birds

Books:

Baicich, Paul J. and Colin J. O. Harrison. *A Guide to the Nest, Eggs, and Nestlings of North American Birds.* 2nd ed. Princeton, NJ: Princeton University Press, 2005.

Burnie, David. *Bird.* DK Eyewitness Books. New York, NY: Dorling Kindersley Publishing, Inc., 2008.

Ehrlich, Paul R., David S. Dobkin, and Darryl Wheye. *The Birders Handbook: A Field Guide to the Natural History of North American Birds.* New York, NY: Simon & Schuster/Fireside, 1988.

Kelly, Irene. *Even an Ostrich Needs a Nest: Where Birds Begin.* New York, NY: Holiday House, 2009.

Laubach, Christyna M. and René, and Charles W. G. Smith. *Raptor!* North Adams, MA: Storey Publishing, 2002.

Winer, Yvonne (author) and Tony Oliver (illustrator). *Birds Build Nests.* Watertown, MA: Charlesbridge Publishing, 2002.

Online Sources:

The Cornell Lab of Ornithology: http://www.allaboutbirds.org/guide/search
National Audubon Society: http://www.audubon.org
Aerodynamics of Animals—Birds—Beginner, AVkids.com: http://wings.avkids.com/Book/Animals/beginner/birds-01.html
The Earthlife Web—All about Birds: http://www.earthlife.net/birds/
Enchanted Learning—Bird Watching: http://www.enchantedlearning.com/subjects/birds/Birdwatching.html
Smithsonian National Zoological Park—Birds for Kids: http://nationalzoo.si.edu/Animals/Birds/ForKids/default.cfm

Fun Bird Words to Learn

Anting: An odd behavior in which birds pick up single ants or small groups and rub them on their feathers, or spread their wings and tail and sit on top of an anthill. The biting ants may reduce skin parasites or help stop itching caused by new feather growth.

Breed: To lay eggs and raise chicks.

Brood: The baby birds that hatch from a clutch of eggs.

Camouflage: Patterns or colors that help an animal blend in with its surroundings in order to protect the bird from predators.

Clutch: The number of eggs laid by a female bird and incubated together at one time.

Colony: A large group of birds (often seabirds) that live together in one place to breed or roost.

Decoy nest: A fake, unused nest, made to confuse predators.

Dominant: A bird that is socially prominent—more powerful or important in the group than the others.

Egg tooth: A horny growth on top of a baby bird's bill; the bird uses it to break out of its shell. The egg tooth falls off soon after hatching.

Fledgling: A young bird that has left the nest.

Habitat: The natural home of an animal, such as forests, parks, wetlands, or grasslands.

Hatching muscle: A strong neck muscle that helps the baby chicks crack the egg open from the inside.

Incubate: To keep the eggs warm, usually at a constant temperature, so that the chick can grow inside. Most birds sit on eggs to keep them warm. Usually, the larger the bird, the longer the incubation period (the shortest period is eleven days; the longest, eighty-one days).

Migrations: Regular, often seasonal, journeys that some birds make to nest or find food.

Molt: To lose old feathers and grow new ones in their place.

Nestling: A baby bird that is still in its nest and can't fly.

Nocturnal: Active at night and asleep during the day.

Predator: Animals that hunt other animals for food.

Raptor: A bird of prey, a predator. They usually have talons (sharp, curved claws), hooked bills, and keen eyesight and hearing.

Roosts: Places where birds rest or sleep. Many birds gather in groups or large colonies—this provides warmth and protection from predators.

Species: A particular type of animal or plant.